THE WARLOCK'S STAFF

SPIKEFIN
THE WATER KING

With special thanks to
Stephen Chambers

For William

www.beastquest.co.uk

ORCHARD BOOKS
338 Euston Road, London NW1 3BH
Orchard Books Australia
Level 17/207 Kent St, Sydney, NSW 2000

A Paperback Original
First published in Great Britain in 2011

Beast Quest is a registered trademark of Beast Quest Limited
Series created by Beast Quest Limited, London

Text © Beast Quest Limited 2011
Cover and inside illustrations by Steve Sims © Orchard Books 2011

A CIP catalogue record for this book is available from
the British Library.

ISBN 978 1 40831 320 6

1 3 5 7 9 10 8 6 4 2

Printed in Great Britain by CPI Bookmarque, Croydon

The paper and board used in this paperback are natural recyclable
products made from wood grown in sustainable forests. The
manufacturing processes conform to the environmental regulations of
the country of origin.

Orchard Books is a division of Hachette Children's Books,
an Hachette UK company

www.hachette.co.uk

SPIKEFIN
THE WATER KING

BY ADAM BLADE

ORCHARD

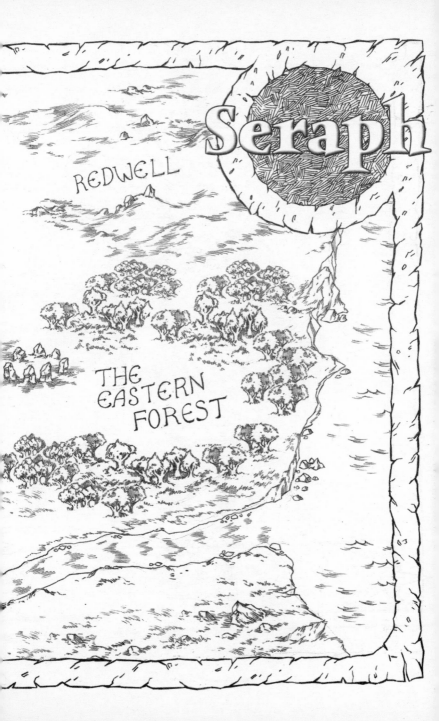

Tom and Elenna are such fools! They thought their Quests were over and that my master was defeated. They were wrong! For now Malvel has the Warlock's Staff, hewn from the Tree of Being, and all kingdoms will soon be at his mercy.

We travel the land of Seraph, to find the Eternal Flame. And when we burn the Staff in the flame, our evil magic will be unstoppable. Tom and Elenna can chase us if they wish, but they'll find more than just Beasts lying in wait. They're alone this time, with no wizard to help them.

I hope Tom and Elenna are ready to meet me again. I've been waiting a long time for my revenge.

Yours, with glee, Petra the Witch

PROLOGUE

It's been a long day, Brenner thought. *But a good one.* He climbed out of his fishing boat and tied it to the wooden jetty. Squinting into the sun that sparkled on the Sea of Seraph, Brenner smiled. The ocean looked like a sheet of rippling blue glass.

Brenner had grown up by the sea. He loved the salty air, and the sound of the waves splashing and rocking his little boat. There was something peaceful about being alone on the water.

His arms were sore and tired as he began unloading the wooden crates of fish from the boat. It was a good haul of sea trout and striped bass – plenty to take to market. Brenner could just see the villagers' faces – they'd be impressed by this catch!

As he hefted the last crate onto the jetty, a shadow fell over him. Brenner spun around. A man in a long dark cloak leant on a gnarled staff just a few paces away.

"Sorry," Brenner said. "You startled me!" He held out his fist, smiling. But the stranger didn't knock his knuckles against Brenner's fist in the traditional Seraph greeting.

I wonder where he is from? Brenner thought. The stranger's stare made him uncomfortable.

In the sunlight, the old man's

face was pale, like sickly fish-flesh. Still leaning on his staff, the stranger drew a rosewood wand from his pocket. The wand's handle was shiny with ivory-coloured points. Scraps of fur were twisted around its leather thongs.

Those are teeth, Brenner realized. *The ivory points are animal teeth.*

The stranger noticed Brenner staring. He looked back to the wand, seeming deep in thought. Then he put it back in his pocket, his alert gaze never leaving Brenner.

It's odd that I didn't hear him approach, thought Brenner. *The jetty should have creaked.* "What can I do for you?" he asked.

The old man's skin stretched across sunken cheeks in a narrow smile, his teeth yellowed like old parchment.

"I would like to buy some fish."

Brenner knew that something about this was wrong. The old man hadn't stopped watching him – hadn't even glanced at the fish crates. His hands trembling, Brenner knelt to open the nearest crate.

"All right," Brenner said. "Which fish would you—"

"Pick three," the stranger interrupted.

Brenner handed him three fish and the old man slipped them under his cloak. "There," Brenner said. "What kind of payment can you make?"

"Here's my payment," the old man said, and he smiled again. He cast his staff aside and drew a slim, vicious-looking dagger from inside his cloak.

The old man lunged, dagger raised. Brenner scrambled backwards, falling

into the shallow water. He stumbled
to his feet and ran towards shore,
splashing in the low waves, his
legs pumping.

Brenner risked a glance over his
shoulder. The old man was gone! The
jetty was empty. "Where did he go?"
Brenner wheezed, slowing down.

"Over here."

Brenner turned around, just as
a hand closed around his throat. It
was as cold as marble. Somehow, the
stranger had appeared in front of

him. But how could that be possible?

As Brenner tried to wrestle himself free, the old man swept his free arm in a low arc, his dagger slashing at Brenner's leg. Before he could even scream in pain, his attacker shoved him under the surface of the sea. Salty water stung his eyes as he tried to rip the old man's grip away.

But he was too strong.

"Now, you belong to me," whispered the old man. Brenner froze, his struggles weakening. How could he hear when he was underwater? It was then that he realised – he had not heard the words through his ears.

The old man's voice was in his head.

Terror turned to rage in Brenner's chest as he flailed again, kicking and punching underwater. But he was growing weak. His vision spotted black. The light began to fade, and he felt his strength draining away, like the pumps failing on a sinking ship. As the light went out, he tasted sea water in his throat, and felt it fill his lungs.

Suddenly, he could breathe again. Still submerged, Brenner's throat was free, and he opened his eyes: the water was pale blue, as clear as winter air. He took a slow breath and looked up at the shimmering daylight. *I can breathe…but how?* He tried to stand and slipped sideways: his legs had turned to a grey shark tail. *This can't be real!* He recoiled, and his tail slapped a cloud of sand at the ocean bottom, jolting his torso to the surface.

The daylight was blinding white.
Water sluiced from silver scales on
his chest and stomach – his body was
covered in them, and his arms… He
held them up to the light. Spikes
jutted out like bone daggers through

16

his skin. He felt gills along the sides of his throat. The surface air was thin, as if he were at the top of a mountain. Looking towards the shore, he felt hot fury in his chest when he saw the cloaked old man.

"Tell me your name," the old man said.

No name, the creature realized. Surging anger clouded its thoughts. *My name…?*

Grinning, the old man raised his staff. "Go forth, Spikefin, Water King!"

CHAPTER ONE

FIRE IN THE MOUNTAINS

"We're getting close," Elenna said.

She rode behind Tom on Storm's back. As they neared the lip of a steep ridge, Tom tugged on the reins. The black stallion stopped and Tom rubbed the arrowhead-notch of white between Storm's eyes.

"Not close enough," Tom said.

They had stopped at a forest

clearing on a cliff, overlooking an evergreen valley that rose to the high mountain peaks of Seraph. As the sun set, Tom saw a faint red light in the distance. *The Eternal Flame*, he thought. It flickered eerie crimson in the mountain-mist. *The goal of our Quest – the one place in Avantia where the dark wizard Malvel can burn the Warlock's Staff.*

"We're not close enough," Tom said. "If Malvel reaches the Eternal Flame first—"

"We'll beat him there," said Elenna. "We won't let him destroy the Warlock's Staff. There's too much at stake."

"Everything is at stake," Tom said. "Malvel will destroy Seraph, and Avantia will pass into darkness. And then Aduro will be dead forever.

We're so close to the end, but I feel like something is waiting for us. A Beast in the mountains, maybe – or worse."

"We'll defeat it," Elenna reassured him. "Aduro's tokens will help us."

Tom nodded, but did not feel any more confident. At the start of their Quest, Aduro gave them six magical tokens, but Tom never knew which one to use next. He was relying on luck as much as skill, and he did not like it. He had used four of them already, and now had just chainmail and a dagger.

Behind them, a voice called, "Why are we stopping?"

Tom looked back. Petra's hands were still bound together by a rope that trailed from Storm's saddle. behind Elenna. Petra was Malvel's

witch apprentice – but he had
abandoned her. She shook greasy
locks of black hair from her eyes
as she frowned at the far-away
light.

"Is that where we're going?" she

22

said. "It's too far. We should rest."

"It isn't up to you," Elenna said. "What do you think, Tom?"

Behind Petra, Tom spotted Elenna's beloved grey wolf, Silver. *He looks back to normal*, Tom thought, relieved. On their last Quest, Malvel poisoned Silver, transforming him into a Beast. But now, he was restored.

"My feet are tired," Petra said. "I don't get to ride on the horse like you two."

"We should stop," said Tom. "It's too dangerous to continue in the dark. If we're attacked, we won't have any warning. And these mountain passes are uneven – Storm could get hurt."

Elenna said, "I suppose this is as good a place as any to make camp."

They dismounted, and began to

23

collect firewood. Elenna disappeared among the trees a little way downhill.

"I could help," Petra called. "If you untie me."

Tom smiled grimly. "Nice try," he said.

Petra huffed. "I don't serve Malvel anymore."

"Prove it," said Tom. "You said you could tell us secrets that would help us defeat him. We're listening."

"Fine," said Petra. "I know that Malvel is weakening. The closer he gets to the Eternal Flame, the heavier the Warlock's Staff becomes. Also, the evil wizard's Black Unicorn, Noctus, is afraid of fire. It won't fly close to the mountain. Malvel will have to complete his journey on foot. It will be very tough for him."

As Elenna returned with firewood, Tom said, "I want to believe you, Petra. After everything that's happened, we could use some good fortune." He glanced back to his friend. "Should we untie her?"

"No," Elenna said. "I think that's a bad idea. Help me with the fire."

Together, they found a pair of black, flinty stones. In the near-darkness, Elenna crouched over the firewood. She banged the rocks against each other again and again, but it was no use – the rocks wouldn't spark. Tom rubbed his hands together as a chilly mist fell over the ridge. The flints were too damp.

"Let me try," he said. "Maybe—"

"My magic can make fire," Petra said, and she smiled.

Elenna drew her bow, nocking an arrow. "If we untie you..."

"I promise to be good," said Petra.

Silver growled at the witch as Tom went to check her wrist-bonds. Storm shuffled closer, his hooves clicking. Tom found the end of the knot, then stopped. *Can we really trust her?* he asked himself.

"Yes, you can," said Petra, as though reading his thoughts.

Tom hesitated, feeling his stiff, tired legs and his empty stomach. *We need to rest if we're going to be strong enough to defeat Malvel, he told himself. And having a tied-up prisoner will slow us down.*

He reached for the knot again, thinking hard. *But she may betray us the first chance she gets...* He shot a look to Elenna, who shrugged as if to say:

I don't know what to do, either.

Tom took a deep breath. Then he untied the knot. "There," he said. "You're free."

CHAPTER TWO

A DIFFICULT CHOICE

Petra rubbed her wrists and glanced at Elenna. "Calm down," Petra said. "Unlike your mutt there, I don't bite."

Elenna lowered her bow and arrow. "Just light the fire."

"Of course." Petra turned closer to Tom. "I just need one thing…" She lunged for his sword, and he sidestepped, his hand on the hilt.

"Not so fast!" Tom shouted.

Petra burst into laughter. "Look at you! You really thought I was trying to take it!"

Tom exchanged a nervous look with Elenna. Petra had reached for his sword. If he hadn't expected it, she might have grabbed it first.

"Light the fire," Tom said, "or I will tie you back up…"

Petra closed her eyes and raised one hand. She whispered, "Glimmering light – break this night!"

A bolt of orange light shot from her palm, striking the logs. They ignited in a sudden snap of fire. The flames were an unnatural shade of green.

"Green fire!" Tom gasped in disbelief.

"Who cares?" said Elenna, sitting

close. "The flames are still warm."

Tom huddled beside her to warm his hands. Petra sat on the other side of the fire. Silver sat by Elenna, while Storm stood nearby as if he was a sentry.

"Tell me, Petra," said Tom. "If you can use your magic to help people, why don't you?"

Petra watched the fire. "Why would I want to?"

"Because it's the right thing to do."

The Witch laughed and looked at Elenna. "Is he like this all the time? He must be so annoying."

"Tom's right," Elenna said. "You have a choice. You could be good."

"Good?" Petra said. "I should be more like you? And then what – follow the mighty Wizard Aduro? What happened to him, I wonder?"

Tom clenched his fists over the fire, trying to stay calm. "We're going to recover the Warlock's Staff," he said. "Then I will return it to its rightful place in the armoury. After that, Aduro will be brought back to life." *I hope*, he thought.

"You're more deluded than I thought," said Petra. As Tom watched her across the fire, shadows played and danced on her cheeks. "Aduro is dead. He's never coming back. That's what goodness has given him."

Tom shivered and looked away. *What if she's right?* he thought.

"It's late," Elenna said. "Let's all get some rest."

"You're not going to retie me, are you?" Petra asked.

Tom thought about it. *If we keep her free, it shows that we're not afraid. But I just don't trust her.*

"Yes," Tom said.

Petra sighed as he bound her wrists again. "Wait, Tom—"

"It's late," he said, and he tugged the knot tight. "Let's just go to sleep."

One hand on his sword handle, he rolled onto his side, away from the fire. *But how will I ever sleep?* he thought. *Malvel is out there. The Eternal*

Flame is so close. How will I...

When Tom opened his eyes again, clouds shrouded the valley and mountains in thick, grey fog. The morning sunlight was thin and pale. At the edge of the cliff, Tom stared at waves of solid mist, as if the world had been covered in a blanket to hide the Eternal Flame. He unfolded the map Aduro had given them. The kingdom of Seraph was full of painted rivers and mountains that dropped in a long strip, surrounded on both sides by the sea. The valleys, ridges and coastlines were dotted with tiny pictures of houses – Villages, Tom thought – all the way down.

"Tom," Elenna said. "Look!"

As they watched, an image appeared on the map.

"It's a silver fish," Elenna said. "Like the kind explorers draw on charts of the deep ocean, to show where no one has been – or to warn them away."

"It must be warning us away," Tom said. He ran his finger along the picture. "It would take us off-course from the Eternal…"

Tom's words died away as, below the fish, letters slowly faded in, like water-spots on the tapestry: *Spikefin*.

Tom gasped. "It's the next Beast!"

Behind them, Petra cackled. "Well, well, well… I believe this is what people with consciences call a 'dilemma'. Which way do you go? Do you continue on your Quest to the Eternal Flame, and let this Beast wreak havoc? Or, do you play the hero and risk letting Malvel get too far ahead of you?"

Tom looked at Elenna, seeing that his friend looked as uncertain as he felt. What were they going to do?

Petra had said Malvel was travelling on foot and growing weaker. If she was right, Tom might just have enough time to stop the Beast and get to the Eternal Flame before the evil wizard. But how much energy would he and Elenna have after yet another battle with a Beast?

Tom looked back to the map, thinking hard. "Fishermen live along the coast," he said. "They could be seriously hurt by the Beast..." He nodded determinedly. "We have to stop Spikefin."

Elenna shook her head. "The Eternal Flame is in the mountains," she said. "We saw it last night. Isn't stopping Malvel and recovering the Staff more important? That's why we're here. If we lose, none of this will matter. The fisherman will still be hurt by Malvel's magic if he gets the power he seeks."

Tom put a hand on her shoulder. "We have never left innocent people at the mercy of Beasts," he said. "We won't start now."

Petra came over to them. "We'll move faster if I'm free."

"No," Tom said. "That rope stays on until I know we can trust you."

Petra scowled and stomped away.

This has to be the right choice, Tom thought. *If I'm wrong, the whole Quest could be doomed.*

CHAPTER THREE

FAST WATER, SHARP ROCKS

Tom studied the map with Elenna and found a curly blue line that wound out of the mountains, all the way to the fish-picture at the coast. It was called the Raging River.

Elenna smiled ruefully. "Why can't it be called the Calm River?"

Tom checked the map again, then pointed south. "It looks like the fastest way to the coast. We might have time to conquer this Beast before we beat Malvel to the Eternal Flame. It's that way – come on!"

They climbed onto Storm and when the stallion trotted on he yanked Petra behind them. Silver sprinted ahead to check the path to the river. As they followed the mountains down, the cliffs dropped into rolling hills, with patches of white stone protruding through a floor of pine needles. Broken stone walls criss-crossed the forest.

"This must have been farmland long ago," Tom commented.

Elenna nodded. "These walls would have marked the boundaries that separated one field from the next."

Tom pointed at a mound of abandoned logs. "Someone once

tried to rebuild and gave up."

Behind him, Petra groaned.
"You two are so boring."

Tom didn't answer. Instead, he
spurred Storm to trot a little faster,
making Petra have to run to keep up.

"No!" screamed the Witch. "Stop it!
I'm going to fall!"

Tom pulled on the reins, slowing
down Storm. Elenna was laughing.
Tom did not have to look behind him
to know that Petra was not.

By mid-morning, they reached
a gorge full of evergreen trees that
sloped down in a field of scattered
boulders, all the way to a foaming
rush of white water and sharp rocks.

The Raging River.

"Let's build a raft," Tom said.

"There's no easy path to the coast and the river will get us there quickly."

He and Elenna found a nearby log pile and tried to roll them to the riverbank. The logs were heavier than they looked and were overgrown with ivy. Even shoving together, Tom and Elenna could only move them in slowly. By the time they had enough to form a large, flat square, Tom was sweating and exhausted. *But there's no time to lose*, he thought. *We have to go. And to build a raft we need rope…*

And the only rope Tom had was around Petra's wrists.

As Tom untied Petra, Elenna asked, "Are you sure about this?"

"We need the rope," he said, as he freed the Witch. Petra rubbed

her sore wrists.

"That's not what I mean," said Elenna. "I mean that." She pointed at the rapids. Water splashed and surged around rocky outcrops, as sharp as talons.

"We're too slow with Petra walking," Tom said, "and Storm can run faster with one rider."

"But—"

"You'll ride Storm along the side of the river. I'll take Petra and Silver on the raft. It's the only way."

"All right," said Elenna, although

she still looked reluctant.

She helped him lash the logs together. When they were out of rope, Tom tested the raft with his foot: the logs were wobbly and uneven, but the ropes were taut and strong.

It will have to do, he thought.

He found two more long sticks. They weren't much use as oars, but they'd at least be able to push away from rocks. He tossed one to Petra. "Here – make yourself useful!"

Together, the three of them dragged the raft to the water. The fast-moving current caught the raft, and Tom jumped aboard. Silver leapt on beside him. The river started to pull the raft away. Tom grabbed Petra's hands and he yanked her on.

The raft spun. Water splashed over the edges and through the log-gaps,

but the raft held together. Tom saw
Elenna, already galloping Storm
along the riverbank. *I hope she can
keep up*, Tom thought.

The raft bucked. Tom crouched
between Silver and Petra. They were
picking up speed. Low-hanging
branches passed near the shore.

"Kneel at the back!" Tom shouted
over the roaring water. "It's going to
pull us down!"

Ahead, the water dipped into a rapid
whirlpool, surrounded by jagged black
rocks, like a bubbling mouth of knives.
As they hit the edge, the front of the
raft started to dip. "Back, back!" Tom
shouted, seeing Petra about to slip off.

Silver growled, his claws clamped
into the wood. Tom and Petra put all
of their weight on the rear of the raft,
which dived in a splashing burst, and

then spun through the whirlpool. The raft tipped forwards but didn't flip over.

The rocks surged closer – Tom jabbed his stick and pushed off, but there were more behind them. "Watch out!" Tom shouted over the river's roar. Petra blocked with her stick, launching them out of the whirlpool, back into the current.

They were all drenched. As Silver shook his wet fur, Tom laughed in relief. "We made it! You pulled your weight back there, Petra! I didn't know if I could trust you earlier—"

"Oh no, Tom," Petra said. "Look!"

Wiping water from his eyes, Tom squinted: ahead, the river vanished. He heard Elenna shout from the riverbank: "Tom, look out!"

He started to turn, and saw a blur

of motion before pain flared in the side of his head. He slumped to the floor, the whole world spinning.

Petra had hit him with her stick!

His vision blurred, Tom saw Petra jump up to catch a low tree branch and pulled herself up as Tom and Silver passed underneath her on the raft.

Tom's head was ringing as he

watched Petra get further and further away. She was now sat astride the branch, pointing and laughing.

Tom sat up shakily. The river was moving too fast, all the way to the edge, where it disappeared.

"A waterfall..." he mumbled.

The sticks were gone. Tom scrambled to the raft edge with Silver, trying to figure out how he might survive. The riverbank was too far away for them to swim in this powerful current.

The edge of the falls rushed closer. Tom ducked, holding tight to the raft. Beside him, Silver scratched the logs frantically, as if he were searching for an escape tunnel. As they went over the edge, the wolf let out a long, desperate howl.

A thrill of terror clenched Tom's

stomach as he watched the river disappear into a cascade far below. The drop yawned and, as the falling water rushed him over, Tom could not see or hear. Some part of him, deep inside the marrow of his bones screamed: *This cannot be how my Quest ends!*

CHAPTER FOUR

A DEADLY SHADOW

As he went over the falls, Tom pushed himself off the raft. He tumbled, flipped, and crashed underwater. The air exploded from his lungs in a cloud of bubbles, and the shield on his back slammed into rocks. *Sepron's tooth!* Tom thought, and as the current dragged him along the bottom, he called on it. Instantly,

the Sea Serpent's talisman got to
work – the water receding away from
Tom on all sides, as he and Silver
floated up to the surface. Breaking
through, Tom took a deep, wonderful
breath.

He tasted salt on the air. He looked
around. This wasn't a river: there
were waves in every direction. Gulls
cawed and drifted overhead.

I'm in the Sea of Seraph, Tom thought, as he treaded water. Silver appeared beside him, paddling in a circle. Tom patted his head. "No more rafts," he said, with a chuckle.

Behind him, the waterfall dropped down a sheer cliff. Skinny trees clung on either side to a rock face of black stone. At the top of the cliff, Petra appeared. She crossed her arms angrily. "Curse it!" she yelled. "Why won't you just *die*?"

"You're going to regret this!" Tom shouted back. "We gave you a chance!"

Tom swam with Silver toward the rocky shore. He spotted Elenna leading Storm down a steep hillside path. When Elenna spotted Petra, she drew her bow and arrow. "Traitor!" she shouted.

Petra sneered down at them. "Do you really think you can hit me from there?"

"Stop!" Tom shouted at Elenna. "She's not worth it!"

Petra stepped back. "This has been fun," she said. "But, as much as I would love to stay and watch Malvel's new Beast kill you, I have more important things to do."

I was wrong, Tom thought. *Petra is not serving Malvel – she only looks out for herself.*

"This isn't over!" Tom shouted. "While there's blood in my veins, I'll make sure you pay for this!"

As Petra disappeared behind the cliff, Elenna carefully guided Storm down the slippery rocks alongside the waterfall. "Are you all right?" she called.

"I'm fine," Tom said, as he swam to the beach. The magic of Sepron's tooth ensured that he and Silver were not swallowed alive by the sea. Further down the shore, he saw a rise of blocky buildings along a curl of hills overlooking a harbour. Sun glared off the orange roof of a wooden villa that stood on stilts in the centre of the harbour. Fishing boats lolled at the nearby docks, but there was no sign of any people.

"There's a village," Tom said, treading water.

Elenna led Storm along the rocky shore. She was frowning at the sea, ignoring the village, eyes narrowing. Then she gasped and pointed behind him: "Look out!"

A huge shadow passed under Tom, moving towards the beach – towards

Silver. Tom struck out, paddling and kicking with all his strength but, before he could reach Elenna's wolf, the water between them seemed to explode. A band of glistening grey scales broke through the surface. *This is Spikefin*, Tom thought.

"Silver, watch out!" he shouted. But it was too late. The water surged under Silver in a fast, unnatural wave, lifting and hurling the wolf into the shallows, closer to shore. The band of grey scales, which Tom now knew was an enormous fish-tail, thundered back under the surface. The blurred, shadowy shape swam toward Silver.

"No!" Tom yelled. "Stay away from them – fight me! I'm your real enemy!"

The shadow turned in a wide arc.

Tom held his shield in his left hand and drew his sword with his right. He held it as high as he could. *I won't be able to make clean strikes*, he thought, with a shiver of dread. *Not when I'm up to my chest in water!* But he had to do something. He'd been in tough spots like this before, and he always came through. He could not let this Beast defeat him – not when he knew that Malvel was out there somewhere, getting closer and closer to the Eternal Flame.

A distorted human head splashed out of the water. It was stretched into veiny ridges that trailed fronds of dark green seaweed hair. White gills pulsed on either side of its neck. As it rose over Tom, water streamed down rows of thick scales that covered its body. The Beast was at least four

times his height. It raised strong
arms – protruding with jagged spikes
of bone – that ended in clawed
fingers. The Beast wheezed and
groaned, as if it were in pain.

Gripping a black, three-pointed trident in its left hand, the Beast watched Tom with pale, lidless eyes.

Spikefin whipped the trident down. Tom barely had time to raise his sword, the impact of steel on steel rattling his arm, the force driving him underwater. He splashed back up, spitting water. The Beast opened its long jaw in a grimace of bone and pink flesh to reveal three rows of serrated shark teeth. Spikefin roared with a deep, wet snarl that shook Tom's ribcage.

Then he lunged again!

CHAPTER FIVE

SPIKEFIN ATTACKS

Tom dodged backwards to avoid the strike, but he was too slow. The Beast caught his shield in its jaws, clamping down and then throwing back its head. Tom was lifted right out of the water. He kicked at the air, yanking at the shield to pull it free, but it was no use. *Crunch!*

One of Spikefin's teeth broke through the wood.

Impossible! Tom thought. *My shield is made of enchanted wood – nothing can break it!*

Spikefin swung his trident, and Tom blocked, catching the prongs on his blade's edge, before flicking it at the Beast's head. Spikefin, his jaws still clamped on the shield, ducked and pulled Tom into the water with him.

Twisting underwater, Tom kicked the Beast's trident away. He placed the sharp edge of his blade against Spikefin's torso, dragging it as hard as he could between the scales.

The Beast recoiled in a bubbling hiss and tore free. Kicking to the surface, Tom saw Spikefin swimming away, surging powerfully through the murky depths. A moment later, it was gone. His arms shaking and tired, his lungs burning, Tom swam to

shore. Elenna helped him out.
Dripping wet, he sat on a rock
covered in broken seashells.

Storm nudged Tom's shoulder with
his head, and Tom smiled wearily.
"I'm all right," he said.

Elenna crossed her arms beside
Silver, who climbed onto the rocks

and shook droplets of water from
his fur.

"I've never seen a Beast fight like
that," Elenna said. "Spikefin is unlike
anything we've faced before."

"I know," said Tom. "And I was
unprepared, because of Petra."

"Do you think she was planning
to double-cross us all along?" Elenna
asked.

"Maybe," Tom said. "Malvel might
have left her behind to win our trust,
until she found the right moment to
betray us. We won't make that
mistake again."

He lifted his shield: there was a
semicircle of gashes where Spikefin's
teeth had dented the surface.
Turning it over, Tom saw that one
of Spikefin's teeth was stuck in the
wood. It had cut all the way through.

Carefully, he wiggled it loose. It was shaped like a razor-sharp triangle, almost as large as his palm.

"How can I battle a Beast if even my shield is useless?" he asked. "No Beast has ever—"

He heard a noise behind him and spun around. Two men were staring at them from the tree-line. The first man was old and grizzled, maybe the father of the second man. They were both thin and sunburnt, wearing worn, wind-tattered clothes.

Fishermen, Tom thought.

"Please, come away from the water," the older man called. "It isn't safe."

"The ocean," Tom whispered to Elenna. "They're afraid of it."

When Tom and Elenna went closer, the men raised their hands, knuckles out. This was how people greeted each other in Seraph. Tom knocked his fist against theirs, and Elenna did the same.

The younger man pointed at Tom. "We saw you out there, fighting that Beast. Please help us. Brenner, our old friend—"

"Best man in the village," the other man added. "He could catch fish in the middle of a hurricane."

"He's missing," the younger man said. "But we don't think he's lost at sea. I found his boat tied to the dock, as neat as always." He nodded to the older man. "Tell them what you saw, father."

The man paled. "I was returning from the market," he said. "I saw something floating in the shallows, near the docks, like brown seaweed.

It was Brenner's clothing, torn to ribbons, bloody and…" He shook his head. "How are we supposed to feed our families with that monster out there?"

"The Beast must have killed Brenner," the younger man said.

Tom glanced at Elenna, and they exchanged a knowing, uncomfortable look. *We've seen this before*, Tom thought. *If Malvel is behind this, then that ruined, hulking Water Beast didn't murder Brenner. It* is *Brenner.*

"Please," the older man said. "You should meet our village leader, Varra. She'll know what to do."

"We'll help however we can," Tom said.

With Silver and Storm, they followed the fishermen along the coast to the harbour village. Wooden houses perched along the rocky overlook in a jumble of sun-bleached walls and arched rooftops crowded by seagulls and pelicans. A stray cat wandered down narrow, steep-cut steps that wound between the buildings to a wide path at the dock. These were simple people, who lived and depended on the rhythms of the ocean. *Without the sea*, Tom thought.

What are fishermen supposed to do?
Malvel's evil could ruin them.

The younger man pointed at the villa Tom had seen in the bay. "Varra lives there."

They left Storm and Silver at the harbour road with the bag containing their remaining magical tokens. Silver settled on top of the bag in the sun, already nearly dry, and Storm watched Tom go, still tense and alert.

The fishermen led them to steps at the end of the dock that rose to the villa's main level. It was shaped like a squat, square box, ringed with a roofed balcony. Wooden roof slats were painted orange, and the wall-logs were streaked salt-white all the way around.

Tom knocked, and a woman with short dark hair answered the door.

She was strong and tall, with chapped lips and bright blue eyes. "Who are these people?" she asked the old man.

"The boy fought the Beast," the grizzled man said. "We think they can—"

"Did they kill it?" she snapped.

"No…"

"Then what good are they? I don't have time for this."

When she tried to slam the door, Tom caught it with one arm.
"Please," he said. "My name is Tom, and this is Elenna. We want to help." He extended one fist.

The woman stiffened. Reluctantly, she touched her knuckles to his in the Seraph greeting.

"I am Varra," she said. "Come in, strangers."

Tom and Elenna followed Varra inside. Outside, the villa had looked mysterious and regal, but inside the rooms were heaped with old nets, hooks, and lobster traps. Everything was cluttered and smelt of metal and fish. The walls were decorated with weapons and objects Varra had probably hauled from the sea: a bronze wheel, a steel helmet encrusted with barnacles, and rows of sharp spears, tridents, and thick, weighted nets.

She noticed Tom examining the weapons and said: "When I was young, I hunted sharks." Varra rolled up her sleeves: her hands and arms were splotched with ugly white scars. "Now what do you want? I don't have time for lies, and I don't have the patience for strangers. The last stranger was

a bad omen." She shook her head, as
if angry with herself. "I knew there was
something wrong about that wicked
old man with the staff."

Tom shared a worried look with Elenna.

"You saw an old man here?" Elenna asked.

"After Brenner disappeared," said Varra, "I saw him wandering the harbour in a dark cloak. That's when all of this started."

"That sounds like Malvel," Tom said. "He's an evil wizard, and if he came here, then he's responsible for the Beast in the ocean."

"How do I know you're not responsible?" Varra said.

"You said he was leaning on a staff. Did he need it to walk?" Elenna asked.

"I think so," Varra replied. "Why? Is that important?"

It might be, Tom thought. *Maybe Petra was telling the truth about some things. Maybe Malvel is getting weaker…*

The room jolted in a sudden thump, as if it had been hit by a tidal wave.

Tom caught his balance on the wall, as the house shook in a crash of spears, hooks, and furniture. He stumbled out of the door onto the balcony. Below, the water thrashed around one of the villa stilts.

"Spikefin!" Tom cried, as the Beast emerged from the rushing, foamy water. He raised his long, deadly tail and drew it back.

Tom turned and ran back into the villa. "Run!" he yelled.

Behind him, Tom heard a *whoosh* before the whole villa shuddered. Spikefin was battering at the stilt again with his tail. Varra's home began to tilt sideways.

How many more strikes from the Beast could it withstand before it collapsed into the sea?

CHAPTER SIX

THE WRATH OF SPIKEFIN

"Do you have a net?" Tom asked Varra.

She pointed to a heavy black net hanging between silver spears. "That one – it's a whale net!"

"That might work," said Tom, as he and Elenna took it down. They helplessly hopped and bounced on the shuddering floor. Something groaned outside, like the sound of an ancient tree trunk breaking. *The stilts are about to snap*, Tom thought. "Get the villagers away from the docks!" he told Varra.

Varra hesitated, but when the room tilted again, she raced out the door.

More wall-hangings crashed and slid down the floor. The floor was steep now, like a hill leading up to the wall – which was where the ceiling used to be. One hand on the net, Tom dragged himself up the slanted floor, reaching up to grab the doorframe. Elenna was right behind him.

"Hold on!" Tom shouted, but it was too late. The room juddered and fell. Tom slid backwards down the floor with chairs, tables, and wall hooks banging around him.

Water burst through the doorway,

surging over him.

Tom splashed to the surface, among bobbing furniture. The villa had fallen sideways into the ocean, and it was filling with water as it sank. Elenna was using a broken chair-back to stay afloat. Luckily, they had managed to hold onto the net.

"Hurry," Tom said, and he nodded to the underwater doorway. "If we swim out with the net between us..."

"We'll catch Spikefin," Elenna said. "Ready?"

Instinctively, Tom moved to hold up his shield – but he had lost it in the fall. And if he had no shield, he did not have Sepron's tooth. This meant he could not manipulate the water. "We'll both have to hold our breath," he told Elenna. "If it's too much, swim back to the surface."

"I'll be careful," she said. "Don't worry."

They took deep breaths and dived. Underwater, the room was dark. Spears, tables, and a wooden statue of a knight drifted past. Tom pointed to the doorway, Elenna nodded, and they pushed off, side-by-side, each holding one side of the net.

Where are you, Spikefin? Tom thought, as they passed out the doorway into the open ocean.

Elenna caught his hand and pointed – there!

A shadowy shape hurtled towards them. In the saltwater blur, Tom saw the Beast's body beating back-and-forth. It came closer and closer, picking up speed. As Spikefin barrelled toward them, his eyes rolled back white, like the killing eyes of a shark.

Tom kicked right, and Elenna swam left, stretching the net tight between them. Spikefin slammed into it. He yanked back, thrashing in confused swipes with his barbed arms.

We've got him! Tom thought, straining to hold on as he and Elenna swam towards each other, closing the net.

In one motion, Spikefin scythed his spiked forearms, slicing open the net. Elenna kicked toward the surface. *Too slowly*, Tom realized. *She'll never make it!* Spikefin turned to her and snapped his jaws, a long sliver of net still trailing from his teeth. The Beast pounded his tail, knifing after Elenna. Tom swam up, grabbed the end of the net hanging from Spikefin's jaw and tugged hard.

The pull of the net jolted Spikefin sideways, and Elenna reached the surface. The Beast dived past Tom, its huge body rippling with jagged spikes and muscle, like an armoured shark. The force jerked Tom's arm, dragging him down. His fingers were caught in the net! Spikefin plunged deeper into black water.

Tom's lungs began to burn. Bubbles burst from his mouth and nose. His vision spotted. Still, Spikefin pulled him down.

Tom twisted, trying to pull free. His fingers came loose, the net scratching and tearing at his skin. But Tom didn't care. He could see the half-submerged villa. He kicked hard as he swam for it, trying to ignore the throbbing of his chest. He knew he could not hold on for much longer.

He swam through the open door of the villa and broke through the surface, sucking in as much air as he could. He coughed and retched as he reached out for a floating table. Blood from the gash on his fingers left bright trails in the water, which was slowly filling the room. *I have to get out of here*, he thought. *It will attract sharks.*

He spotted his shield lying face up between a pair of rusted lobster traps. He grabbed it, as Elenna appeared beside him, still clinging to her chair-back.

"Tom," she called, "are you all right?"

"I'm fine," he said. "But the Beast is stronger than I expected. We have to plan our next move quickly, before—"

The water erupted under him.

Spikefin burst to the surface with his mouth gaping teeth, his trident aimed at Tom's throat.

CHAPTER SEVEN

BAITING THE BEAST

Tom splashed backwards as Spikefin stabbed his trident past Tom's chest. The Beast's mouth gaped open, his serrated teeth glistening. Tom swiped his sword at Spikefin's head – but the Beast easily dodged.

As Spikefin drove the trident at him, Elenna lunged and grabbed it with both hands. His jaws snapping fast,

Spikefin turned to bite her, and Tom
jabbed his sword into the Beast's
mouth. Still out of the water, Spikefin
roared in pain, and Elenna yanked the
trident away. She fell backwards
across a floating cabinet.

Spikefin swung his bladed arm at Tom
as he tracked him to a shallower corner

of the room. Pale gills flexed and wheezed on the Beast's neck. Spikefin's eyes rolled white again.

"Hey! Fish-face! Over here!"

Elenna was shouting behind the Beast to distract him. Spikefin spun, and she stabbed the trident between the scales in his belly. The Beast reared back, arms slapping the water in anger in panic. He made a hoarse, wheezing sound and pawed at his wounded gut.

He can't breathe, Tom realized. *Spikefin can't survive out of the water!* He slid his shield around and raised his sword, ready to make the winning strike.

Spikefin dived over Elenna like a breaching whale and crashed back underwater in a white spray that knocked them both backwards.

The Beast was gone.

Tom and Elenna climbed out of the villa window, where they sat on the wall and caught their breath.

"What are we going to do?" Elenna gasped.

"We have two magical items left," said Tom. "A dagger and the suit of chain mail. But which one will help us defeat Spikefin?"

Elenna looked about herself. "Let's get to the shore," she said. "It'll be easier to make a decision when we're not looking over our shoulders for the Beast the whole time."

"Good idea," said Tom.

Together, they swam for the beach. Varra was waiting with a crowd of fisherman, and Storm and Silver. Silver ran to Elenna, and Tom patted Storm's side as he stepped out of the

waves. The fishermen stared past
Tom at the broken villa. It looked like
a shipwreck. One upper corner and
a row of windows still rose above the
water as it slowly sank into the bay.

"What do we do now?" asked Varra.

"You do nothing," Tom said. "But
we're going to finish this." He opened
Storm's saddlebag and took out the
shiny black dagger and the chainmail.
He set the magical items side-by-side
on the dock.

"You're going to kill the Beast?"
a fisherman called out.

"No one is going to die," Tom said.
"Unless I'm very wrong, Malvel's
magic has transformed your friend
Brenner into that Beast."

"No!" a fisherman said.

"That's impossible!" a second one
call out. "How can that be?"

I need to do something quickly, Tom thought. They're starting to panic even more. He stared at the two magical items. If he picked the wrong one, his Quest was over. He wished that there was a way to test the tokens before using them.

Then he realised that there was a way. Spikefin's tooth was embedded in his shield – what would it do to the chainmail?

Tom pulled Spikefin's shark tooth from his shield and carefully dragged it across the chainmail links. Nothing – not even a scratch!

This chainmail must have magical qualities, Tom thought. *Somehow, it's even stronger than my shield. But how can I use it?*

As the frightened fishermen muttered among themselves, Tom

studied the tethered fishing boats, nets, poles – a plan was beginning to form in his mind.

Elenna crouched beside him. "What are we going to do?"

Tom looked back out to the ocean. Somewhere out there was a wounded, angry Beast that needed to be defeated. "I'm going to be Beast-bait," he said.

Behind him, the fishermen burst into protest.

"No, you can't!"

"That's madness!"

"It's the only way," Tom said, standing up and turning to them. "In the water, Spikefin is king. We can't fight him out there. If I can lure him onto land, we might defeat him." He handed the dagger to Elenna, and lifted the chainmail suit. It was gossamer-thin, with tiny links like rock-hard wax paper. "And this chainmail is going to give us the best chance."

"I don't understand," Elenna said. "The chainmail will protect you, yes, but Spikefin is too strong. You said it yourself."

"I only need to sink," Tom said. "I told you, I'm going to play dead. With Sepron's tooth token in my shield, I won't drown. This chain mail is the only thing we have that can withstand Spikefin's jaws."

"But you're still hurt," Elenna said, gesturing at his bloody hand. There were gashes in his chest and leg too.

"Exactly," Tom said. "The blood will draw him to me."

Elenna was still shaking her head, but the others were quiet, as if waiting for instructions. Tom unfolded the chainmail and dropped it over his shoulders. It unrolled down his waist. He slipped his arms into the heavy sleeves. Strange – the chainmail was much heavier than it looked.

"Can you swim when you're wearing that?" Elenna asked.

"It's a risk," he said. "But, while there's blood in my veins, I have to try."

CHAPTER EIGHT

THE DEADLY OCEAN

Storm stomped and snorted when
Tom stepped onto the docks, and
Tom smiled back at his stallion.
"Don't worry," he said. "I'll be
right back."

Elenna and Varra led the fishermen
after Tom to the end of the jetty. The
steps that had risen to the villa had
been smashed, and the shredded

scraps floated around the edges of the submerged house.

Tom spotted a long coil of mooring chains piled on the jetty. "There – we'll tie that chain around my waist," he said, winding it tight over the chainmail. Tom hooked one end and handed the other to Elenna. "When I yank on the line, pull me out," he said. "All of you will need to help."

The fishermen formed a line, passing the chain back so they could all hold it. Tom stepped to the edge of the dock. The water was deep and dark blue. *Every moment, Malvel moves closer to the Eternal Flame*, Tom thought. *But there is nothing else for it. Spikefin must be stopped.*

Tom moved towards the edge of the dock, and Varra touched his shoulder. "This is no ordinary sacrifice," she said. "Our people will always remember your bravery, Tom."

Beside Varra, Elenna smiled, and Silver and Storm watched from the shore. Storm raised his head high, as if he were proud of his rider.

Tom took a deep breath – he knew he might have to hold it for longer than he ever had before. Then he dove off the dock.

He hit the water hard, the weight of the chain making him sink and sink, until he felt it tighten. He was at its end.

Tom was suspended in the dim water. He squinted and saw curls of red blood drifting and spiralling up from his hand and leg. His pulse pounded, thudding loud in both ears.

Show yourself, Spikefin!

A dark shape appeared in the

distance, its tail beating slowly back and forth. It wasn't Spikefin. As Tom watched, the shadow drew closer, a second one soon joining it. And then a third.

Through the murky water, Tom recognized the dorsal fins on their backs. Sharks! They circled at the edge of his vision, gliding high and then low, as if they wanted to smell their meal before they tasted it.

Should I yank the chain or should I wait?

Tom let his right hand drift down to grab his sword hilt, and with his left he touched the shield strap.

If they attack at the same time, he thought, *I won't stand a chance.*

A shark surged close, tipping its head back to angle its mouth toward Tom's head. Tom twisted the

shield around and slammed its nose.
The shark jolted back, its tail
flailing. *Behind me!* Tom spun and
blocked a second attack. The third
shark chomped at the sea, its teeth

grazed Tom's armoured shoulder. They were pressing close, eager now.

Tom turned back to block another shark, but it darted past his shield and bit his armoured arm. He couldn't even feel it through the chainmail. Tom beat his sword against its nose, and the shark swam away.

I'm too slow in this chainmail, he thought.

Now there were more sharks circling below him, angling toward his legs, but they pulled back. The sharks scattered, swimming into the ocean darkness.

What's happening?

A giant shadow floated towards him. The water was so still that in the murky darkness, Tom saw tiny bubbles clinging to its interlocking scales. It raised jagged arms and watched him with white menacing eyes.

Spikefin had arrived!

CHAPTER NINE

HOLD ON!

Tom let his body hang slack in the ocean current. Spikefin passed on his right, circling him, his scales shimmering in slivers of daylight that drifted through the sea.

Come on! Tom thought. *What are you waiting for?*

But Spikefin held back, baring his teeth and flexing his claws.

This isn't going to work, Tom thought.

Spikefin knows I'm trying to trick him.

Just as Tom reached to tug the chain, Spikefin surged towards him. Tom braced himself. The impact knocked the air from his lungs. The Beast's jaws clamped on Tom's chest. The links of chainmail stretched and twisted around Spikefin's teeth, but they did not break.

Spikefin's head was close, and Tom could see that his pale eyes were full of malice. He was more animal than human now. Tom worried that there might be nothing he could do to restore Brenner to his human form.

Spikefin jerked back, shaking Tom in a blinding blue-black blur of bubbles. Tom grabbed the slippery fins on either side of the Beast's head. Spikefin's jaws clamped tighter, thrashing left and right. Waves of pain tore through Tom's torso.

Tom had to grit his teeth to stop himself from crying out. If he did, he would release the deep breath he had taken – and then his Quest would be over. He tried to yank Spikefin's head back to pry open the Beast's mouth, but it was no use. Spikefin was too

strong. In another moment, the Beast would crush his ribcage!

Tom's mouth filled with the metallic taste of blood. *I can't fight like this… I have to get free…*

The chain around his waist tightened. He was drifting upwards – Elenna and the others were pulling him out! Spikefin realized it, too. The Beast's mouth slackened, but his teeth were caught in the chain mail. Tom held onto Spikefin's head fin as they broke the surface.

As Tom was pulled out of the water, Spikefin came out after him, like a fish caught on a hook. The Beast dangled and writhed, his jaws still stuck on Tom's chest. Spikefin wheezed and gurgled as they were hoisted onto a loading platform at the edge of the dock.

"Now!" Tom heard Elenna shout.

He saw her charge with a crowd of fishermen carrying ropes. Wrestling the slippery Beast, they coiled ropes around its arms and legs. Tom released the Beast's fins, and Spikefin slipped, crashing across the dock in a wet, snarling heap.

"Careful!" Elenna called. "Don't let the Beast—"

Spikefin floundered, launching two fishermen off the side and into the water. The Beast jammed his arms into the planks and pulled himself back toward the edge, dragging Elenna and three fishermen by their ropes.

"No!" Tom shouted, his voice hoarse with pain and breathlessness. "You're staying right here!"

He grabbed the bony side of Spikefin's tail. Barbed points at the tip whipped past Tom's face.

More fishermen rushed to help, roping Spikefin and struggling to pull him down onto the dock, away from the ocean. *The Beast is trying to get back into the water!* Tom thought, and pulled harder on its tail. Elenna tossed a rope that snared Spikefin's throat.

"Now!" she shouted. She and the fishermen yanked the rope. Spikefin was dragged backwards, shredding the dock with his arms as he fought.

Tom stepped over him, still holding the Beast's tail.

"Please…" Spikefin hissed. "Free…"

Tom felt a flutter of hope in his burning chest. He's speaking!

Spikefin's tail was shrinking like wet paper in Tom's hands. The bony studs on his arms were moulding back into human wrists and fingers. The Beast's face flattened. Scales smeared into skin and hair across a sunburnt body. Tangled in seaweed and caked in gritty sea sand, the man collapsed to the dock.

Tom crouched beside the man, who quivered and whimpered. "Brenner?" he said. "Is that you?"

CHAPTER TEN

SECRETS AHEAD

Brenner looked from Tom to his trembling hands, and then at the other fishermen.

"Brenner?" said Varra. She knelt to wrap a tarpaulin over Brenner's shoulders and around his body. "You're safe now. What do you remember?"

"There was a cloaked man," Brenner said, "carrying a staff. He was old, but...strange. I sold him fish, and he..." Brenner's voice wavered. "He chased me into the water. He tried to kill me. That's all I remember."

One of the fishermen pointed at the sunken villa in the bay. The sun was setting on the horizon, lighting the clouds in brilliant purples and oranges. "That happened next. You did that, Brenner!"

"What?" Brenner paled and looked at Varra. "Your house? But how? I don't understand."

"It's all right, Brenner. We are happy to have you back." Varra looked at Elenna and Tom. "These two saved your life."

Brenner nodded at them, his eyes filling with tears. "Thank you."

"You're welcome," said Tom.

"And now you'll both join us

for a feast," said Varra.

As the fishermen cheered, Tom gazed at the sky. The sun cast long shadows over the beach as it sank beyond the horizon. It was almost night-time. *We defeated a Beast and helped these people*, he thought. *But at what cost?*

He looked to Elenna, and could see in her eyes that she was having similar thoughts. There was no way of knowing how much closer Malvel had got to the Eternal Flame.

"I'm sorry," he told the crowd. "But we must be on our way."

The fishermen protested, following as Varra walked them back to shore. "Even if you are in a hurry," she said, "you must eat." She clapped at the fishermen. "The ocean is ours again. The water is safe, and the fish will return. Get a fire going!"

Tom felt Elenna tug at his sleeve. "Actually," she said. "A nice meal before travelling is not a bad idea."

Tom nodded. "But we can't stay long."

As night fell, they grilled fish. The fishermen lit bonfires in the street and played music on whale-bone flutes. With Storm and Silver standing close by the warm fire, Tom ate his fifth fish and drank fresh water from a ceramic mug. The fish tasted smoky and wonderful. Elenna ate four.

"We are heading for the Eternal Flame," Tom told Varra. "Malvel, the evil wizard who changed Brenner into a Beast, is also searching for it."

"We can't let him get there first," Elenna said.

"Your village is safe now," said Tom, as he set down his empty plate. Carefully, he wrapped his wounded hands in thin strips of bandages. The wounds were shallow and clean, which meant that they would heal quickly. "But if we don't stop Malvel, all of Seraph could be destroyed."

"I understand," said Varra, her face grave. "Don't worry about us. We've lasted through hundreds of storms. This is just one more." She pointed up into the dark mountains, where Tom could see a red-orange glow pulsing in the distance, like a bloody star. "That's where you're heading?"

"Yes," Tom said. "Malvel was here only a day ago, and the Eternal Flame is a little more than a day's travel inland, if we move quickly."

"Do you know what you're doing?" Varra asked. "The Flame is dangerous, Tom. We have all seen it – this village was built in its shadow. But we never go near it. Only the strongest, with pure goodness in their hearts can approach. There are very few who would trust themselves to stand in its glow. The Flame twists

the evil inside you to find every dark space in your mind. It knows everything you are, and everything you might be. Do you understand?"

Tom held her gaze. "We have to go there," he said.

Elenna nodded. "We're the only thing in Malvel's way."

"Very well," Varra said. "Do you have a map?"

Tom unrolled the tapestry-map to show her. Varra traced her fingers from the shore to the flame, then back to the empty stub of a mountain.

"There is something missing from your map," she said. "The old mines. They run under this mountain pass. My ancestors built them, in the days when this bay was crowded with trade ships. The mine tunnels will save half a day. We can guide you."

"I'll do it!"

Brenner was watching from the edge of the fire. "It's the least I can do," he said. "They saved my life."

Varra nodded. Tom stood and extended a fist to Brenner. "Thank you," he said, as the fisherman bumped his knuckles. "This is exactly what we need to have a chance..."

Someone giggled in the darkness. In one motion, Tom spun round and drew his sword. A shadow flitted away from the village, disappearing among the dark rocks.

"Was that Petra?" Tom whispered. "It sounded just like her…"

"How could she know to find us here?" Elenna murmured. "Do you think she overheard our plans?"

"I don't know," said Tom. "But if she did, we'll be ready." He clapped Brenner on the shoulder. "Let's go."

Malvel has a head start, Tom thought, *and Petra may know our plan.*

He said goodbye to the fishermen, then climbed onto Storm.

One more Beast to face, Tom thought. *One more token to use. After that, the fight for Aduro, Seraph, and for all the known worlds will really begin.*

Tom spurred Storm into a trot. Silver and Brenner jogged to keep up, as they walked resolutely into the dark Seraph night.

Join Tom on the next stage
of the Beast Quest when he meets

TORPIX
THE TWISTING
SERPENT

Win an exclusive
Beast Quest T-shirt and goody bag!

In every Beast Quest book the Beast Quest logo is hidden in
one of the pictures. Find the logos in books 49 to 54
and make a note of which pages they appear on. Write the
six page numbers on a postcard and send it in to us.
Each month we will draw one winner to receive
a Beast Quest T-shirt and goody bag.

THE BEAST QUEST COMPETITION:
THE WARLOCK'S STAFF
Orchard Books
338 Euston Road, London NW1 3BH
Australian readers should email:
childrens.books@hachette.com.au

New Zealand readers should write to:
Beast Quest Competition
4 Whetu Place, Mairangi Bay, Auckland, NZ
or email: childrensbooks@hachette.co.nz

Only one entry per child.
Final draw: 4 September 2012

You can also enter this competition
via the Beast Quest website: www.beastquest.co.uk

Join the Quest,
Join the Tribe

www.beastquest.co.uk

Have you checked out the Beast Quest website? It's the place to go for games, downloads, activities, sneak previews and lots of fun!

You can read all about your favourite beasts, download free screensavers and desktop wallpapers for your computer, and even challenge your friends to a Beast Tournament.

Sign up to the newsletter at www.beastquest.co.uk to receive exclusive extra content and the opportunity to enter special members-only competitions. We'll send you up-to-date info on all the Beast Quest books, including the next exciting series which features six brand-new Beasts!

Get 30% off all Beast Quest Books at www.beastquest.co.uk
Enter the code BEAST at the checkout.

All books priced at £4.99,
special bumper editions
priced at £5.99.

Orchard Books are available from all good bookshops, or can
be ordered from our website: www.orchardbooks.co.uk,
or telephone 01235 827702, or fax 01235 8227703.

Series 9: THE WARLOCK'S STAFF
COLLECT THEM ALL!

Malvel is up to his evil tricks again! The fate of
all the lands is in Tom's hands...

978 1 40831 316 9

978 1 40831 317 6

978 1 40831 318 3

978 1 40831 319 0

978 1 40831 320 6

978 1 40831 321 3

Series 10: Master of the Beasts
Out March 2012

Meet six terrifying new Beasts!

Noctila the Death Owl
Shamani the Raging Flame
Lustor the Acid Dart
Voltrex the Two-Headed Octopus
Tecton the Armour-Plated Giant
Doomskull the King of Fear

Watch out for the next Special Bumper Edition Grashkor the Death Guard!
OUT JAN 2012!

978 1 40831 517 0